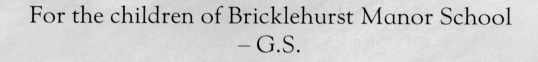

For the children of Bricklehurst Manor School
– G.S.

For my Ema and Mima
– P.L.

An Imprint of Sterling Publishing
387 Park Avenue South
New York, NY 10016

SANDY CREEK and the distinctive Sandy Creek logo are registered trademarks of Barnes & Noble, Inc.

Text © 2013 by Gillian Shields
Illustrations © 2013 by Polona Lovšin

This 2015 edition published by Sandy Creek.

ISBN 978-1-4351-5967-9

Manufactured in Guangdong, China
Lot #:
2 4 6 8 10 9 7 5 3 1
11/14

The Littlest Bunny

Written by
Gillian Shields

Illustrated by
Polona Lovšin

Sandy Creek
NEW YORK

It was spring! The sun was shining, the birds were busy, and the blossom was blooming. Mommy Bunny's babies were playing on the green, green grass.

They were called Bouncy, Fluffy, Snuggly, Cuddly, Jolly, and Polly.

Then, smaller than all the other bunnies,
there was the Littlest Bunny.

The Littlest Bunny longed to bounce as high as his brothers and sisters.

"Watch me!" said Bouncy Bunny.
Hoppity . . . loppity . . . bounce!

"Look at me!" said Fluffy Bunny.
Hoppity . . . loppity . . . bounce!

"And look at me!" cried the Littlest Bunny.
Hoppity . . . loppity . . . hup . . . hop . . .

FLOP!

"You're just too little," the others said kindly. "Don't worry!"
But the Littlest Bunny felt sad.

One morning, the bunnies were playing under a blossom tree. A branch hung low, laden with flowers.

"I'm going to catch some blossoms!" laughed Jolly.
"So am I!" said Polly.

"Me too!" shouted Snuggly, Cuddly, Bouncy, and Fluffy.
Skippety . . . trippety . . . bounce!

When they bounced back down they were covered
in heaps of frilly, frothy, pink flowers.

"Let's give them to Mommy Bunny!"
cried Cuddly. "Come on, everyone!"

But the Littlest Bunny didn't have any blossoms of his own to give.
So he tried very hard to bounce and catch some.

Jumpity . . . bumpity . . . bump!

He tried again.
Skippity . . . slippity . . . slump!

The Littlest Bunny still couldn't reach
the blossoms. He tried even harder.
Flippity . . . flappity . . . flop!

He bumped and slipped and flopped straight into . . .

. . . a tiny brown mouse, who was even smaller than a very small bunny.

"Look where you're going!" said the mouse, smoothing his whiskers and straightening his tail.

"I'm sorry," said the Littlest Bunny. "I was trying to get some blossoms for my mommy. But I'm too little!"

"Then why don't you give her something little?" said the Tiny Brown Mouse. "Little things can be lovely. Just look around!"

So the Littlest Bunny opened his eyes wide and looked.

He saw a dainty acorn cup, a drop of dew,
and a little red beetle on a blade of grass.

He saw a small shiny pebble, a round brown nut,
and a tiny blue feather, so curly and soft.

"They're very nice," said the Littlest Bunny.
"But I want to give my mommy something as big
and special as a heap of pink blossoms."

"Small things are special too,"
said the Tiny Brown Mouse.
"Come and see!"

He ran over to a hollow tree where
white flowers grew like tiny stars in the grass.
"Look!" said the Tiny Brown Mouse.

The Littlest Bunny peered inside the hollow.

There, tucked up fast asleep . . .

. . . were the Tiny Brown Mouse's babies.

"Aren't they beautiful?"
he said proudly.

"Oh!" said the Littlest Bunny.
"They're lovely! And so teeny-tiny."

At last, the Littlest Bunny saw that the world was full of beautiful small things – and that he was one of them too!

"I know what to give Mommy Bunny now," he said.
"Thank you, Tiny Brown Mouse!"

The Littlest Bunny couldn't wait
to get home, and he hurried away
over the green, green grass.

"I know what to give her!" he sang.
"I know, I know, I know!"

When he got home, his brothers
and sisters were playing outside.

"Where have you been, Littlest Bunny?"
they said, rushing up to him.
"I've been looking for something special," he smiled.
And he hopped inside the burrow.

Mommy Bunny was waiting for him.
"There you are, my little one!" she said.

"Look what I've found for you, Mommy!" said
the Littlest Bunny. "It's little, like me!" And he gave
her a single white flower, as bright as a tiny star.

"I love it!" said Mommy Bunny.
"And I love my Littlest Bunny even more!"

The Littlest Bunny was so happy that he had to . . .

. . . hoppity . . . loppity . . .

BOUNCE!